The Race Around the World

by Lilli Henderson

NATIONAL GEOGRAPHIC LEARNING | CENGAGE

Welcome to the race
around the world!
Are you ready to go?

We start the race at the airport in Los Angeles, U.S.A. Here is our first clue!

We're in Mexico City. Look!
There's the flower shop.

This is the right place. Let's get the next clue!

Fly to Rio de Janeiro,
Brazil. Go to the docks.
Find the man who sells fish.
Get your next clue.
CLUE #2
Mexico City
SOUTH
AMERICA
Rio de Janeiro

We're in Rio de Janeiro. There's the man who sells fish at the docks!

We get some fish and a clue.

Fly to Kimberley, South Africa. Drive to Vaalbos National Park. Look for a sign and get your next clue.
CLUE #3
AFRICA
Rio de Janeiro
Kimberley

We drive from Kimberley to the park.
Here we are at last.

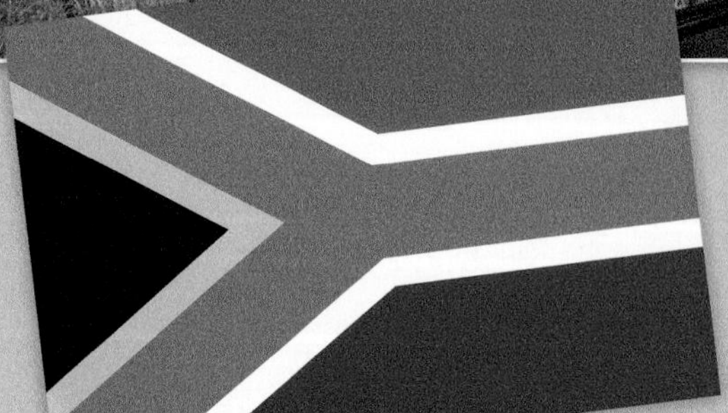

Look at the animal crossing sign.
Our next clue is there.

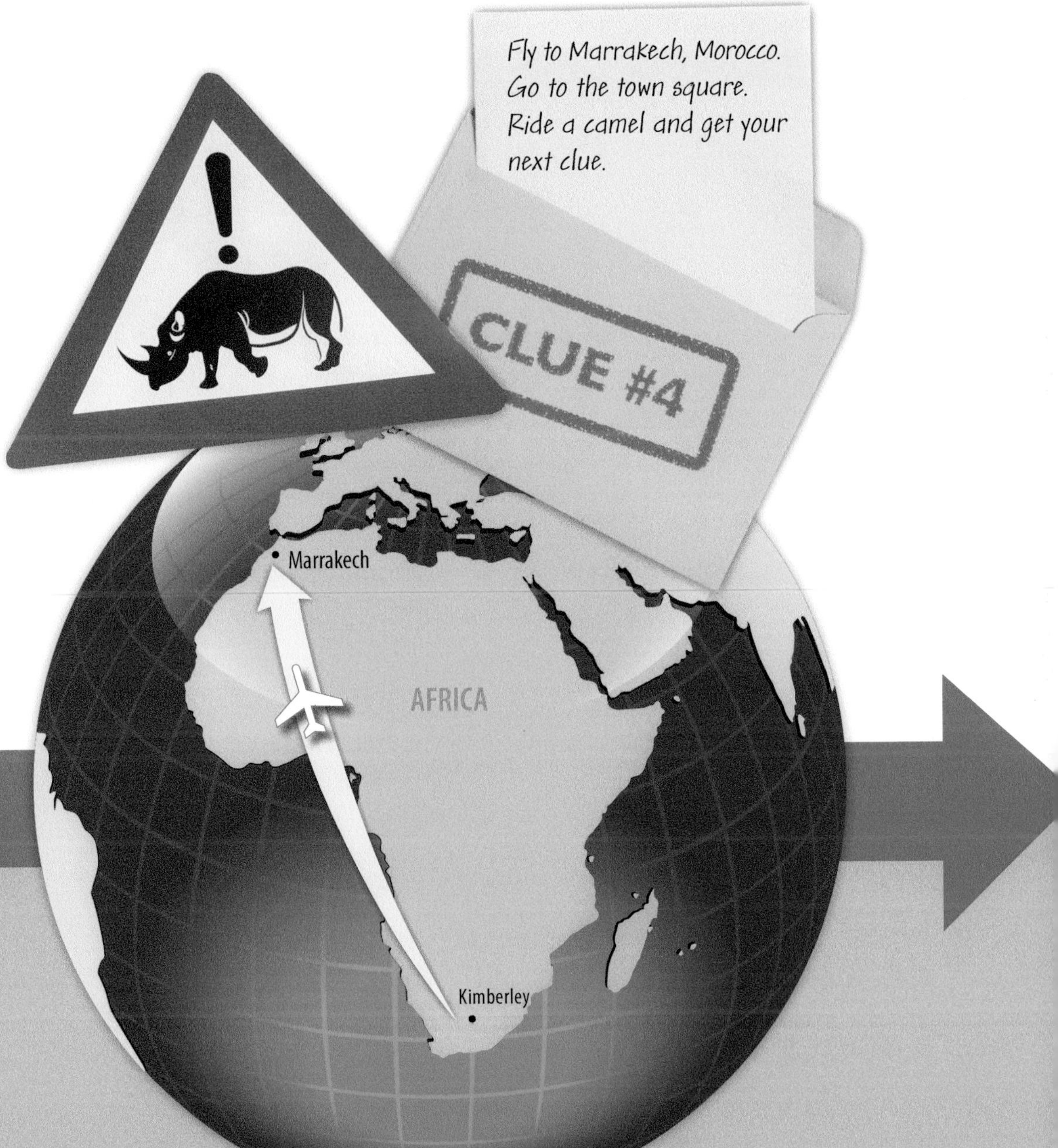
Fly to Marrakech, Morocco.
Go to the town square.
Ride a camel and get your
next clue.
CLUE #4
Marrakech
AFRICA
Kimberley

Now we're at the square in Marrakech.
Let's ride that camel!

What a bumpy ride! But we get our next clue.

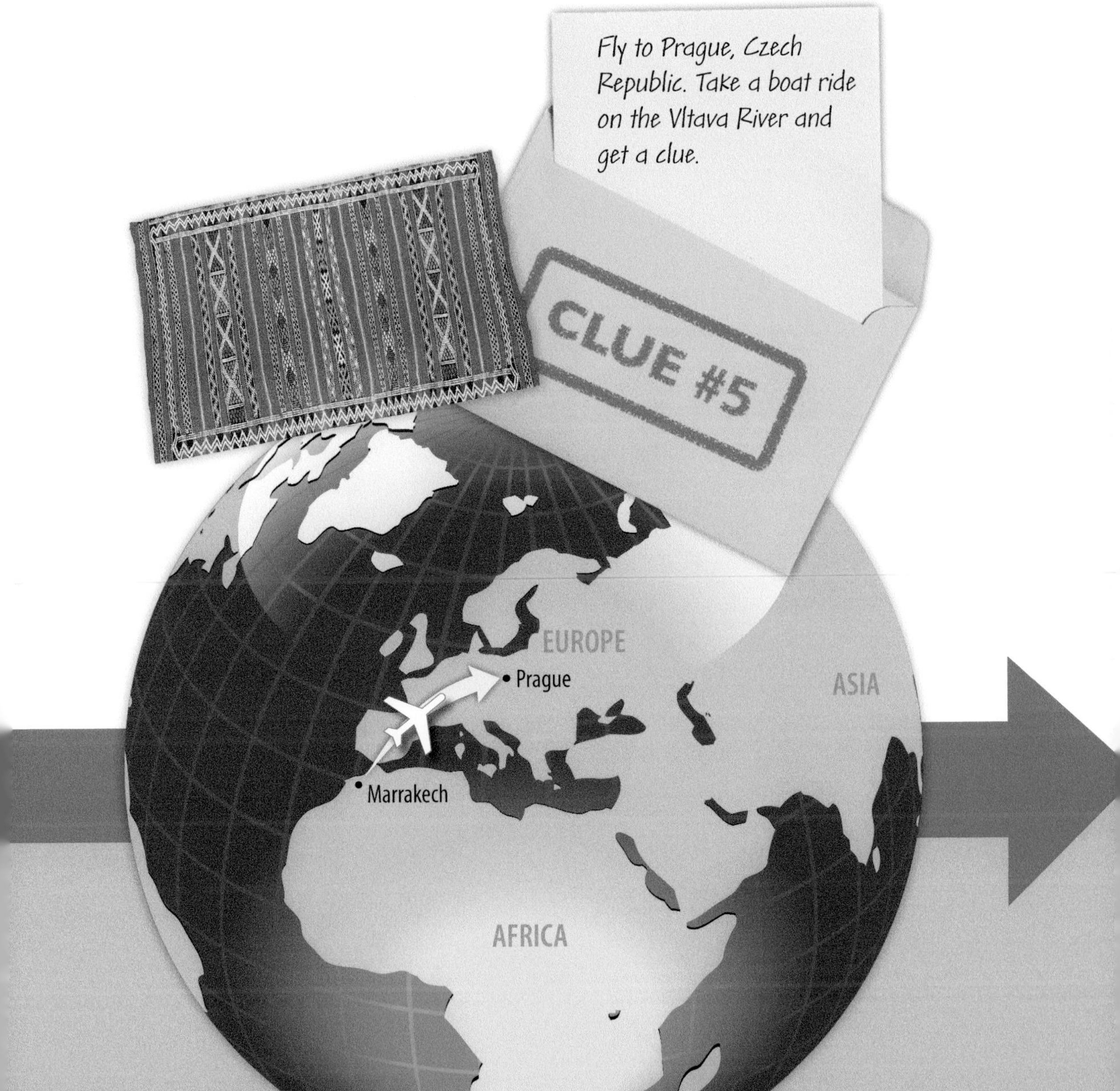
Fly to Prague, Czech Republic. Take a boat ride on the Vltava River and get a clue.
CLUE #5
EUROPE
Prague
ASIA
Marrakech
AFRICA

Prague is a beautiful city. There's the river!

Hurry! We need to get on that boat!
Then we'll get our next clue.

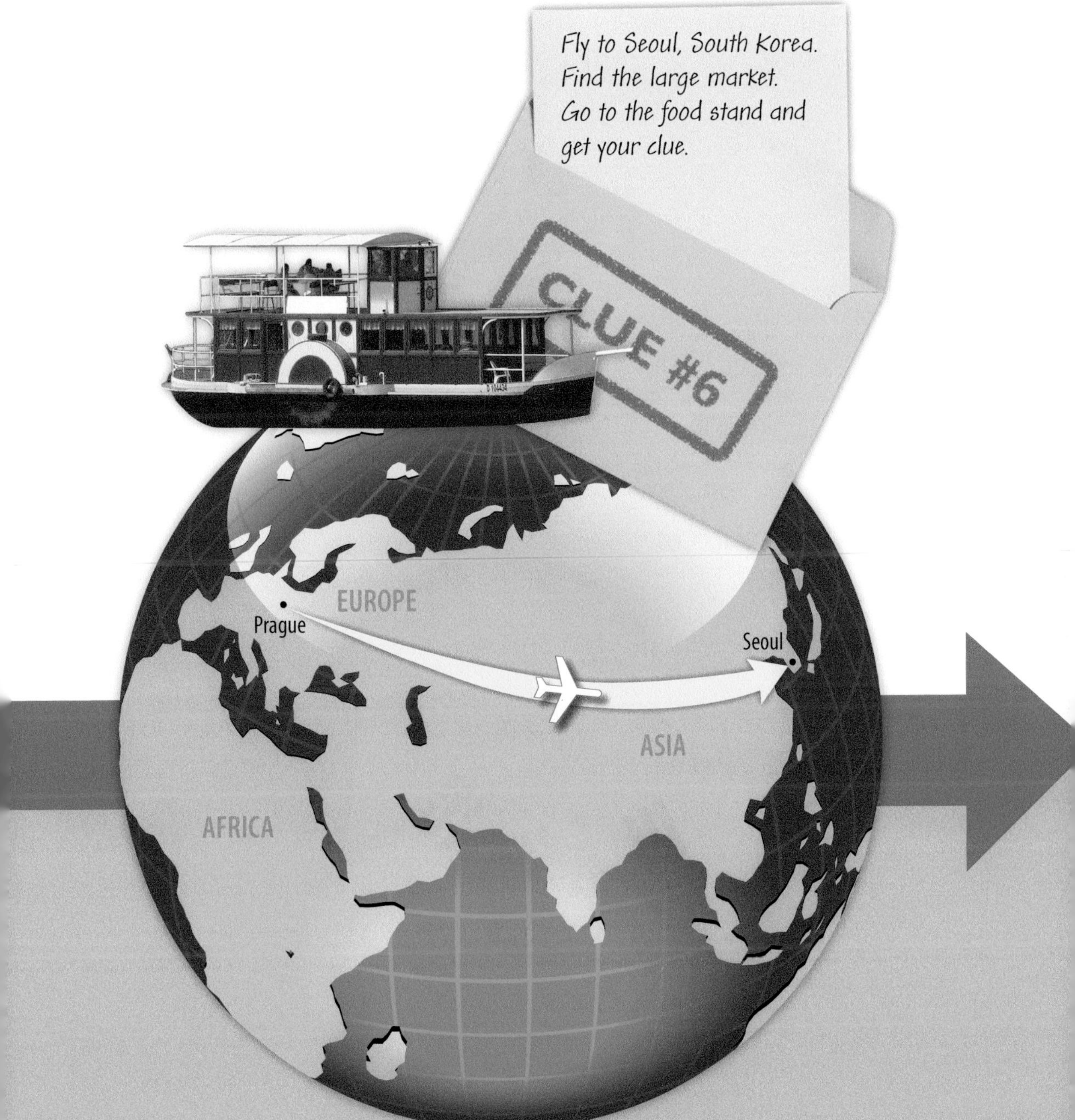
Fly to Seoul, South Korea.
Find the large market.
Go to the food stand and
get your clue.
CLUE #6
EUROPE
Prague
Seoul
ASIA
AFRICA

The market in Seoul is very crowded.
Is this the right food stand?

Yes. Let's get our next clue
(and something good to eat)!

Fly back to Los Angeles. Hurry! You can win the race!
CLUE #7
ASIA
Seoul
Los Angeles

We're back in Los Angeles. We made it around the world!